LITTLE OTTER
Learns to Swim

Written by **ARTIE KNAPP**

Illustrated by **GUY HOBBS**

Little Otter started to quiver.
She was scared of the mighty river.
It was the first time away from her den,
But Mother Otter told her to jump in!

Then Little Otter was having fun,

Splashing about in the summer sun.

Her first swimming lesson was about to begin.

Little Otter's excitement caused Mother to grin.

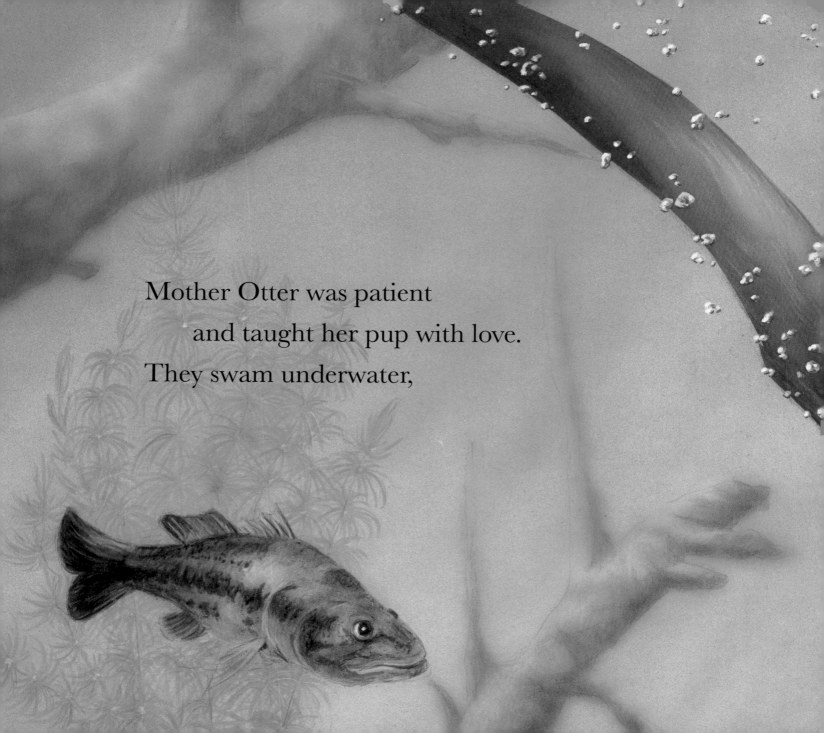

Mother Otter was patient

and taught her pup with love.

They swam underwater,

And floated above.

Diving practice came next,

as Little Otter dove off logs . . .

It's a great way to sneak
up on unsuspecting frogs.

When lessons were done it was time for a rest.
Little Otter lay snug against Mother's chest.

The next few weeks
were more of the same:
Swimming—diving—
and playing water games.

One morning Mother said she'd return in a hurry,
But seeing a bobcat made Little Otter worry.

The bobcat was young, too. It stared and hissed.

Then an eagle swooped down,
but luckily missed.

Little Otter was frightened and dove underwater.
Although afraid, she was a proud otter's daughter.

When she came up, Mother was still away,
So Little Otter ran home . . . to hide for the day.

Mother Otter returned, and listened intently.
She comforted her pup and spoke to her gently.

The river, said Mother, is the safest place to be,
Away from their predators, like wolf and coyote.

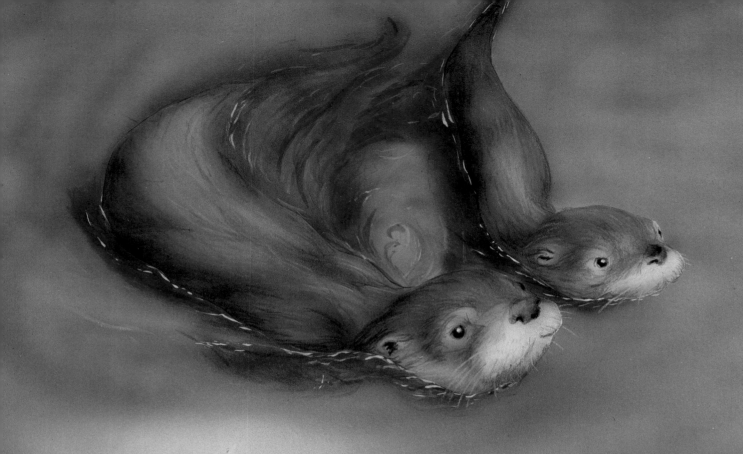

At dawn Little Otter hurried back to the river.
The moon was still lighting the sky with a sliver.

The river was where Little Otter longed to be.
There, she was home, with great company.

ABOUT NORTH AMERICAN RIVER OTTERS

River otters are very important animals, and not only because they're so cool. River otters live on land, but they hunt and travel in the water. That means they need healthy environments to live in, so that they get clean water and good food to eat, just like humans and all other living creatures. If you have river otters living near you, it's a good sign for your environment. Let's make sure we protect our environment for otters and everyone!

- River otters can be found in streams, lakes, reservoirs, and wetlands and along coasts in most states and territories of the United States and Canada.

- River otters are about 3.5 to 4 feet long, including their tails.

- River otters weigh 15 to 25 pounds on average, with males a little heavier than females.

- The main diet of river otters is fish, but they also eat crabs and crayfish, insects, birds, frogs, rodents, and turtles. They go for whatever is slowest and easiest to catch!

- River otters dive to hunt fish, closing their ears and nostrils to keep water out. We don't know exactly how deep they can dive, but we think it's about the same as their cousins, the Eurasian river otters, who dive from 10 feet to 46 feet deep! Dives as deep as 10 feet are much more common.

- River otters usually stay underwater for less than a minute at a time. Although we often read accounts of dives lasting 8 minutes, they are incorrect and are probably based on observations of otters that found air pockets underwater.

- Den sites include hollow logs, log jams, piles of driftwood or boulders, and abandoned lodges and bank dens made by nutria or beaver.

- River otters also den under boathouses, duck blinds, and other human structures up to half a mile away from water.

- River otters usually have 1 to 3 pups but can have as many as 5 in a litter.

- Some animals know how to swim the moment they're born, but river otters learn when they're 1 to 3 months old.

- River otters socialize in groups—either groups of related mothers with their pups or groups of males. A large group of river otters is called a romp or a bevy.

- Humans often destroy river otters' habitat, polluting their water, depleting their fish stocks, and tearing down streamside trees and shrubs for their own convenience or desires.

- The average life span for a river otter in the wild is 10 to 12 years.

You can help NORTH AMERICAN RIVER OTTERS!

Teachers can help students either work together as a class to write a letter or write individual letters to their representatives, offering all the reasons they want to save WATERSHEDS. Healthy watersheds make healthy otter-sheds, for otters, humans, and all of us!

Some states still allow trapping otters for fur. Check to see if your state allows it, and if it does, you can ask your representatives to stop it. Otters need their coats and humans do not!

Visit The River Otter Ecology Project website and discover how we learn where otters are, what they eat, how they move around, and how we can help make sure they do well. Hint: if we make sure they have clean water, lots of fish to eat, and plenty of places to sleep and have their young, they will do fine.

Look on our website for a fun list of 25 ways to help otters.

Don't miss out on our videos and photos, on Facebook and the website.

Page Resource: The River Otter Ecology Project: http://www.riverotterecology.org/
Facebook: The River Otter Ecology Project

Megan Isadore, The River Otter Ecology Project

Megan Isadore is a cofounder and the Executive Director of The River Otter Ecology Project and the Deputy Continental Coordinator for North America for the Otter Specialist Group, IUCN-SSC. She's passionate about wildlife, conservation, art, and children's books, and has worked toward conservation of various species for 20 years, all centering around watersheds.

ARTIE KNAPP is the author of 40 published children's literature works that includes books, videos, stories, and poems. His children's stories have been published in numerous course books by Orient BlackSwan, Oxford University Press, Pearson Education, and The Chart Institute in Japan, among others. Additionally, Artie's work has been published in various magazines and newspapers, as well as online publications. Among his writing credits are the children's books ***Stuttering Stan Takes a Stand*** and ***Living Green: A Turtle's Quest for a Cleaner Planet***, a shortlist finalist for the Green Earth Book Award. He is a member of The Society of Children's Book Writers and Illustrators and graduated from Ohio University. Artie lives in Cincinnati, Ohio, with his wife and daughter. To learn more about Artie and his work, visit him online at www.artieknapp.com.

GUY HOBBS is an artist who specializes exclusively in wildlife art. His paintings are collected internationally, and he has won a number of prestigious awards and accolades. Born in England, he has had a passion for both art and wildlife from a very young age. Guy's first experience of pristine wilderness came when he worked at a safari lodge in the Kafue River Reserve in Zambia, surrounded by stunning riverine forest and some of Africa's most spectacular wildlife. Continuing his love for the wilder places of the planet, he later relocated to the Kootenay region of British Columbia, where he lived for nine years, before relocating to the South Shore of Nova Scotia in 2016. He considers himself very lucky to share his backyard with deer, bears, coyotes, and raccoons—not to mention a huge variety of birds. To learn more about Guy and his work, visit him online at www.guyhobbs.com.

For the memory of my sensei and friend,
Police Officer Sonny Kim, Badge 396.
Artie Knapp

For my wonderful wife Kerry,
thank you for believing.
Guy Hobbs

Ohio University Press, Athens, Ohio 45701 • ohioswallow.com
© 2018 by Artie Knapp • All rights reserved

To obtain permission to quote, reprint, or otherwise reproduce or distribute material from Ohio University Press publications, please contact our rights and permissions department at (740) 593-1154 or (740) 593-4536 (fax).

Printed in Canada • Ohio University Press books are printed on acid-free paper ⊗ ™

Cover art by Guy Hobbes • Cover design by Beth Pratt

28 27 26 25 24 23 22 21 20 19 18   5 4 3 2 1

Library of Congress Cataloging-in-Publication Data
Names: Knapp, Artie, 1973- author. | Hobbs, Guy (Artist), illustrator.
Title: Little Otter learns to swim / written by Artie Knapp ; illustrated by Guy Hobbs.
Description: Athens, Ohio : Ohio University Press, [2018] | Summary: A baby river otter learns to swim, dive, and play in her natural habitat and, encouraged by her mother, begins to explore on her own, learning to escape shoreline predators. Includes facts about North American river otters and resources from the River Otter Ecology Project.
Identifiers: LCCN 2018025206| ISBN 9780821423400 (hardback) | ISBN 9780821446515 (pdf
Subjects: | CYAC: Stories in rhyme. | North American river otter--Fiction. | Animals--Infancy--Fiction. | Rivers--Fiction. | BISAC: JUVENILE FICTION / Animals / General. | JUVENILE FICTION / Nature & the Natural World / General (see also headings under Animals).
Classification: LCC PZ8.3.K713 Lit 2018 | DDC [E]--dc23
LC record available at https://lccn.loc.gov/2018025206